Marlon Bundo's
A Day in the
NATION'S CAPITAL

Written by CHARLOTTE PENCE
Illustrated by KAREN PENCE

Regnery Kids

Regnery Kids™ is a trademark of Salem Communications Holding Corporation;
Regnery® is a registered trademark of Salem Communications Holding Corporation

Cataloging-in-Publication data on file with the Library of Congress

ISBN: 978-1-62157-929-8
e-book ISBN: 978-1-62157-930-4

Published in the United States by
Regnery Kids, an imprint of
Regnery Publishing
A Division of Salem Media Group
300 New Jersey Ave NW
Washington, DC 20001
www.RegneryKids.com

Published in association with the literary agency of Wolgemuth & Associates, Inc.

Manufactured in the United States of America

2019 Printing

Books are available in quantity for promotional or premium use.
For information on discounts and terms, please visit our website: www.Regnery.com

*This book is dedicated to the men and women who
serve our nation in uniform, past and present—
and to their families who sacrifice so much
for our freedom.*

6

Hi, there! Have we met? If not, I'm Marlon Bundo Pence.

I live in Washington, D.C., with my Grandma and Grampa.

You might know them as the vice president and second lady!

There are lots of events here at my home, the Naval Observatory.

Today, we have school children visiting from all over the country!

Grandma used to be a teacher, so she leads them in the Pledge of Allegiance.

Can you say it with us?

I pledge allegiance to the flag of the United States of America and to the republic for which it stands, one nation under God, indivisible, with liberty and justice for all.

7

With one ear raised, I listen to the words of the pledge and I feel a little confused.

What do *liberty* and *justice* mean? How are we *one nation under God*?

Grandma says the Pledge of Allegiance reminds us of all the things that make America special. Justice means treating everyone fairly, and liberty is all about freedom.

8

One of our freedoms is religious freedom, says Grandma, which is why a lot of people came to America.

I hop to the window and look at the National Cathedral down the street.

This is one of the symbols in Washington that stands for religious freedom.

Grandma says there are more places in our nation's capital where we can learn what the pledge means.

Let's hop around and find them!

One of the ways we exercise our freedom is by voting for our elected leaders!

The Pledge of Allegiance says the United States is a "republic," which means that we get to choose who our leaders are.

Look! I can see the Capitol dome!

In this country, we all have to obey the laws, but we are also allowed to have our own opinions about important things. And a place where this right is protected is the Supreme Court!

This is the place that is in charge of upholding *justice* and making sure every American citizen is treated fairly, no matter how rich or poor or young or old you are!

Can you guess how many Supreme Court Justices there are?

We can also learn about important issues and form our own opinions by reading!

When we read about famous people and events from history, we learn important lessons—like how to treat everyone fairly.

A good place to read is at the Library of Congress which has thousands of books—it's the biggest library in the world!

I even found my first book here!

CONSTITUTION
OF THE
UNITED STATES OF A

...B...People...
Article I

We can also learn a lot about our country by looking at historical documents. Some of those are found in the National Archives, including the US Constitution, written more than 200 years ago!

In just four pages, the Constitution spelled out exactly how our country would be run—and how our rights would be protected.

We can see it up close under this glass case!

Oh, look! I can see the White House down the street!

That's where the president of the United States lives, which is the highest elected position in our nation. But the president isn't a king, like in other countries. We get to *choose* our president every four years.

Let's wave hello!

21

We can celebrate our freedom in lots of ways—including the arts!

Plays and concerts are a great way to discover new points of view, and one of the best places to see a play or concert is at the Kennedy Center.

Shh... I think the curtain is about to go up!

Our country had some amazing leaders right from the beginning! George Washington was our first president. He was also a general who fought bravely for America's liberty in the Revolutionary War.

We remember him with this big monument. I think it looks like a pencil!

25

Abraham Lincoln was the president of the United States during the Civil War, and he is known for freeing the slaves with his Emancipation Proclamation. This was an important step in creating justice and equality for all people.

I hop up the steps to say hello, but I don't know if he can hear me all the way up there!

Equality means that all people are treated the same way. That was the hope of another great American: Dr. Martin Luther King, Jr.

He made a lot of important speeches about equality while he was a pastor.

One of the most famous is called "I Have a Dream."

Do you have any dreams for America?

Thousands of people come to Washington, D.C., every year to learn about our nation's history. And if they come in the springtime, they can also see these pretty, pink trees that go all the way around the Tidal Basin.

They were a gift from the people of Japan to the people of the United States in 1912.

Across the water, we can spot the Jefferson Memorial with the round top, honoring President Thomas Jefferson!

Some places in Washington are a little sad, but they are still very important to visit. One of my favorites is the Vietnam War Memorial.

When you walk down the ramp, you can read the names of all the soldiers who fought and died in that war. They are carved into the black marble stone, and people come from all over to find the names of their loved ones.

33

34

When I think of the Pledge of Allegiance, I think of the flag and all the important things the flag and the Pledge stand for—like freedom, justice, and equality.

But then I realize—we don't get these things on our own.

There are people who fight for us to be free every day—like the soldiers from World War II, who raised our flag at Iwo Jima.

Before we go home, there's one more place we need to go.

At Arlington National Cemetery, I see American flags placed at the headstones of each of the soldiers who have given their lives to protect our country and all the freedoms we enjoy.

Today, we learned about the rights and liberties we have as Americans.

We also learned that it is okay to have different opinions. Even when we disagree, we are still *indivisible*, which means we will be one country no matter our differences.

So before we head home, there is one more thing to do.

I bow my head and whisper a tiny "thank you" to these brave souls.

It is because of them that we are able to live in a country that is free—

"One nation under God, indivisible, with liberty and justice for all."

Did You Know?

National Cathedral

If you go outside the vice president's residence, you will see the beautiful National Cathedral. It took eighty-three years to build and was finally completed in 1990. It has 112 gargoyles and 215 stained glass windows. It is the sixth largest cathedral in the world.

US Capitol

The US Capitol is where elected representatives in the House and the Senate vote. It is a key building for the legislative branch of government, which determines which bills and acts turn into law.

Supreme Court

The Supreme Court is the highest federal court of the United States and consists of eight justices and one chief justice. A Supreme Court Justice serves on the Court for life or until he or she retires, resigns, or is removed.

Library of Congress

The Library of Congress is the largest library in the world. It has over 167 million items and about 838 miles of bookshelves. The Main Reading Room has 16,000 titles in about 56,000 volumes all displayed on open shelves.

National Archives

At the National Archives, you can see the United States Constitution on display. It is the document that defines our democracy, and the many articles within it state how our government is set up. It is so important that it has a special glass case it stays in.

The Constitution lists many of our rights and liberties, including freedom of religion, speech, and the press, rights of assembly and petition, and the right to bear arms.

White House

The White House is where the President of the United States and the First Family live. It has 132 rooms, including a red room, blue room, and green room. The East Room is where Lincoln housed the troops, Dolly Madison hung up her laundry, and Amy Carter roller-skated. Lots of performances happen there, and the president gives speeches in this room, too.

The John F. Kennedy Center for the Performing Arts

The Kennedy Center hosts lots of plays, concerts, and shows year-round. At night it is lit up with beautiful lights!

Washington Monument

The Washington Monument is the world's largest stone structure and has fifty flags around it. About a third of the way up, you can see the bricks change colors. That's because construction on the monument was halted in 1854. Twenty-five years later, the workers used different marble when they started again.

Lincoln Memorial

The Lincoln Memorial sits at the end of the US National Mall. You can see it all the way from the US Capitol. A statue of President Lincoln is at the very top of all the stairs. He was the sixteenth president of the United States and was president during the Civil War. On the walls inside the memorial are two of his speeches: the Gettysburg Address and his second inaugural address.

MLK Memorial

The Martin Luther King, Jr. Memorial stands in honor of the Reverend Dr. Martin Luther King, Jr. He and his many speeches and sermons were a key part of the civil rights movement and he worked hard to promote his message of nonviolent protest. The monument depicts Dr. King emerging from two pillars of stone. On the side, words from his speech, "I Have A Dream," are etched into the stone. It reads, "Out of the mountain of despair, a stone of hope."

Jefferson Memorial / Cherry Blossoms

In 1912, Mayor Yukio Ozaki of Tokyo gave 3,000 cherry trees to the city of Washington, D.C. Every year, thousands of people come to see the cherry trees bloom at the National Cherry Blossom Festival. Across the Tidal Basin is the Jefferson Memorial. It honors President Thomas Jefferson, who was our third president of the United States.

Vietnam War Memorial

The Vietnam War Memorial has over 58,000 names of servicemen and women who paid the ultimate sacrifice and gave their lives for freedom in the Vietnam Conflict. When you walk down the ramp into the two-acre national memorial, it is a very somber experience.

Iwo Jima

The Battle of Iwo Jima took place in World War II when the United States landed and took control of the island of Iwo Jima in Japan. The Marine Corps War Memorial (Iwo Jima) is based on a photograph that was taken by Joe Rosenthal of the Associated Press when he saw soldiers raising the flag at the battle. Sculptor Felix de Weldon of the US Navy then created a life-size model of the image, which was later cast in bronze, a process that took almost three years to complete.

Arlington National Cemetery

The Arlington National Cemetery is a United States military cemetery. It is the only national cemetery that has servicemen and women buried there from every war in US history. On Memorial Day Weekend, soldiers place flags in front of every tombstone to pay tribute to those who have given their lives for our freedom.

Sources

National Cathedral: https://cathedral.org/architecture/facts-figures/

Library of Congress: http://www.loc.gov/rr/main/

Washington Monument: https://www.nps.gov/wamo/faqs.htm

Lincoln Memorial: https://www.nps.gov/linc/learn/historyculture/inscriptions.htm

Vietnam Veterans Memorial: https://www.nps.gov/vive/index.htm

Iwo Jima: https://www.nps.gov/gwmp/learn/historyculture/usmcwarmemorial.htm

Arlington National Cemetery: https://www.history.com/news/arlington-national-cemetery-8-surprising-facts